The Nicholas Stories

The Nicholas Stories

The Maiden Voyage Of Kris Kringle

CHRISTMAS, 2004
TO: MARY JOHNSON
A special wish For You!
May God's Light always shine On You!!!
Larry D. Faw

Written by Harry B. Knights

Original Artwork by Calico Studios
Publisher - Larry D. Faw
Zweig Knights Publishing
A Subsidiary of Studio City Holding Corp.

3

Dedication
To my best friend, my wife Chris.

Printed and bound in Mexico

This publication is designed to provide inspiration to young and old, and, is designed in its content for all peoples of the world. It is being published with the understanding that the publisher is not engaged in political intent, and, is being sold to encourage peace and love for humanity.

ISBN: 1-58114-020-5

Cataloging-in Publication Data

Knights, Harry B.
    The Nicholas Stories: The First Flight Of Saint Nicholas
        P. cm.
Summary: A girl's wish was granted and she became known as Kris Kringle and she would travel the world each Christmas Eve with Saint Nicholas and deliver a gift of love to every boy and girl..

[1. Christmas--Fiction. 2. Santa Claus--Fiction. 3. The North Pole--Fiction. 4. Religion--Inspirational. 5. Family Values--Fiction. 6. Kris Kringle.]
  1. Title.

The text type was set in Goudy Oldstyle.
The display type was set in Old English Text and Goudy Oldstyle.
The interior pages were printed on 80# Patina Matte.
The jacket wrap was printed on 100# stock with gloss laminate.
Production photography by Hans Kaczmarek, German Master Photographer and Son.
Color separations were made by Blackhawk Color Corporation.
Printed and bound by R.R. Donnelley & Sons Company.

Prologue

Nicholas Kringle had a very unselfish wish.
He wanted to make children happy.
As a young man, one of his selfless acts of love
was witnessed by angels,
and his wish was granted. He would become
known as Saint Nicholas and travel the world
each Christmas Eve to deliver a gift of love
to every boy and girl.
Then, one day, a doll mysteriously
appeared in The Land Beyond Yon.
Finding the doll startled the Elves.....
But Nicholas knew how to solve the mystery.
This is the continuing story of Nicholas.
I know that it's true, because I was
there... the whole time.

Mouka

In The Land Beyond Yon, Saint Nicholas and the Elves stayed very busy. Each year, there would be more and more children and more and more wishes to fill. This, of course, made Nicholas and the Elves very happy.

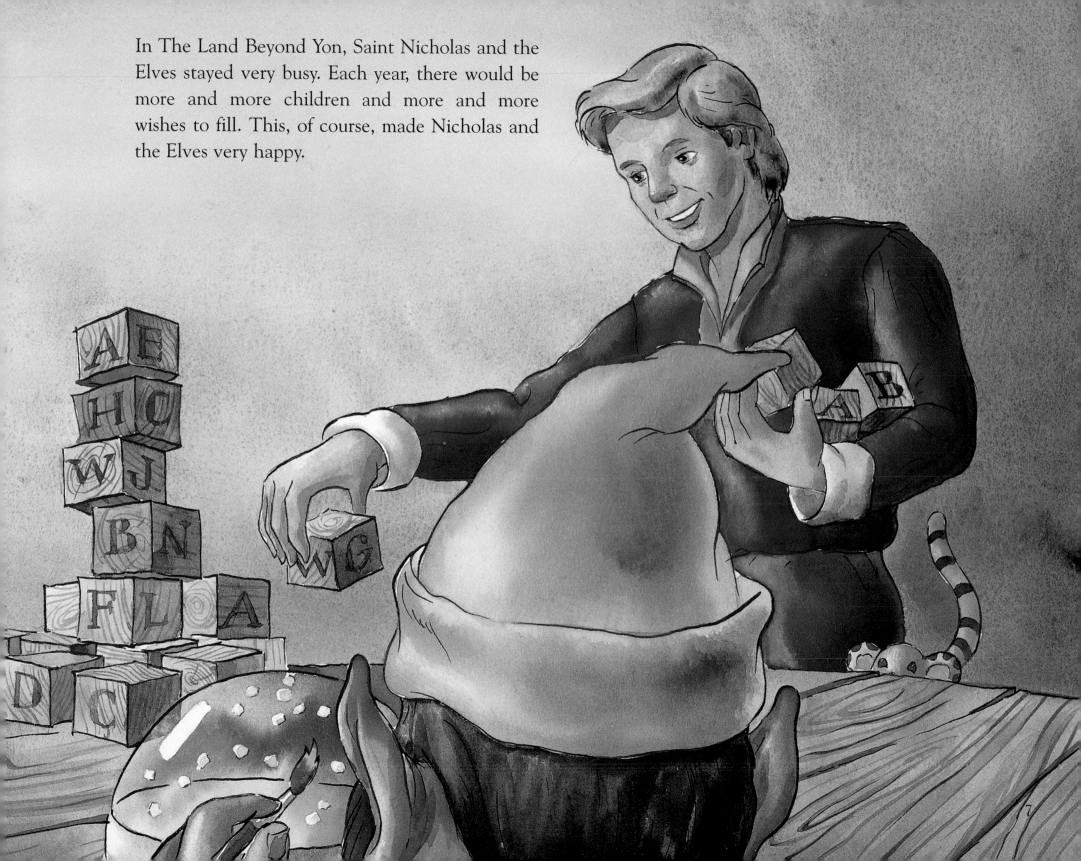

One day, while collecting wood in the forest, Goe found a beautiful doll beside a tree. "Where did it come from?" he wondered. Goe carefully placed the doll inside his jacket and took it straight to Nicholas.

Nicholas recognized the doll right away. He had made it for a young
girl named Kristina, several years ago.

9

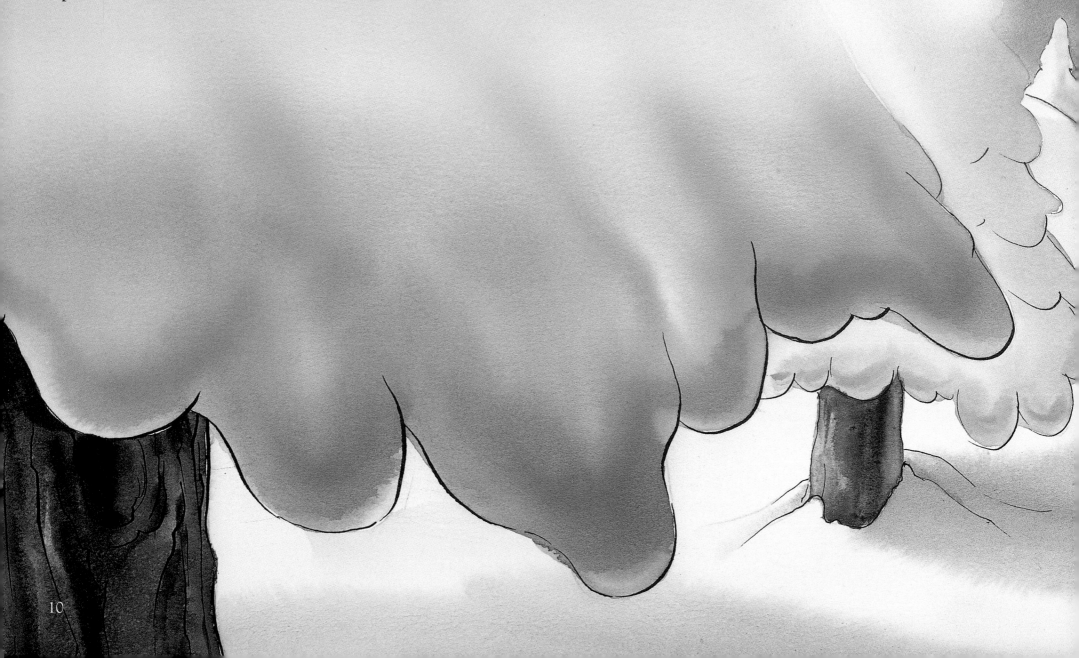

Kristina was very ill at the time. She had been wishing for a beautiful new doll and her father thought that the doll would make her feel better. Nicholas made the doll and delivered it on a stormy night, but on the way home he had a terrible accident. Nicholas knew that Kristina would not be far from her doll, and he asked Goe to take him to the place where he had found it. What he did not know, however, is that the doll had changed Kristina's life.

Kristina was born unable to hear. When she tried to speak, she did not sound like the other children. They teased her and made fun of her. These children made her feel so badly that she seldom tried to speak at all.

She named her new doll Rebecca. She could talk to the doll and, of course, the doll never had anything bad to say to her. Rebecca soon became Kristina's best friend.

Kristina loved to read. For her, reading was a great adventure that took her to all parts of the world. Sometimes she would imagine herself as the captain of a big ship.

Other times, she would imagine that she was a fairy princess. The books were her friends as well as her teachers, and how she loved them. She would read stories to Rebecca every day. All this practice helped the girl learn to speak quite well. In fact, Kristina began to sound just like all the other children, even though she could not hear herself speak.

Whenever a classmate was having a problem, Kristina would be there to help. This was something she really enjoyed doing. It was not long before she had many friends.

Years later, Kristina became a teacher. This was a perfect job for her, because she was surrounded by two of her favorite things in the whole world: books and children. She loved the challenge of helping each and every one of her students, and they all loved her very much.

Kristina's illness never completely left her. Sometimes, it would challenge the girl and she would become very, very sick. These were the times that she would hold Rebecca and her thoughts would return to the boy who made the doll for her. It was her greatest wish to meet Nicholas and tell him how the doll had changed her life. After all, she knew the terrible price the boy had paid to deliver Rebecca to her in that storm so many years ago. Somehow, Kristina would always seem to get well again. However, each battle would leave her slightly weaker.

Then, one day she felt very, very, badly. Her illness was more than she could bear. Kristina had never felt so terribly in her entire life. She held Rebecca as her father stayed at her side. Mercifully, she fell into a deep, peaceful sleep.

That night, something wonderful happened!
A beautiful, bright Light shone through her
window and onto Kristina.

20

She awoke, feeling wonderful. There was no more fever, no more aches, and no more pain. Kristina had never felt so well in her whole, entire life. She sat up as she heard the cooing of a white morning dove. Why, for the first time ever, she could *hear*! The beautiful Light dimmed to a bright sunny day. Kristina wanted to tell everyone what had happened.

However, no one was there. She found herself in a forest. Kristina called out, but no one answered. She decided to start walking to see if she could find someone.

24

Her newfound hearing overwhelmed Kristina. The sound of the wind whispering through the trees, the chirping of birds, even the crunch of snow beneath her feet, were all fascinating new sounds.

Later, she decided to rest for a moment. She sat Rebecca on a small rock. She heard new sounds coming from a nearby tree and she walked over to investigate.

She laughed at the antics of two squirrels.

A few minutes later, she returned to the rock, but Rebecca had disappeared! Kristina was very upset! She frantically began to search for her doll. She saw small footsteps in the snow and decided to follow them.

Sometime later, it began to snow very hard and the wind blew directly at Kristina. The snow stuck to her like glue, and she became covered from head to toe in pure white.

The snow stopped for a moment and the sun shone directly on her. Just then, Nicholas and Goe came around a bend and they stared at her. She was so beautiful that she looked like an angel dressed in white.

"Hello!" said Nicholas as he took Rebecca from his pocket. "You must be Kristina!" This was the very first human voice she had ever heard. She thought it was the most wonderful sound of all. "I *am* Kristina, but who are *you* and how did you know my name?" she asked.

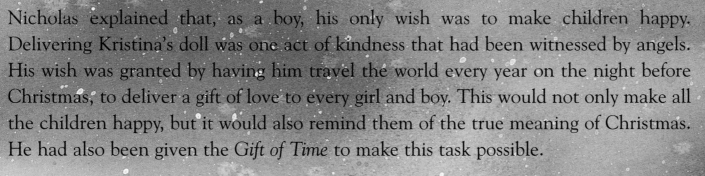

Nicholas explained that, as a boy, his only wish was to make children happy. Delivering Kristina's doll was one act of kindness that had been witnessed by angels. His wish was granted by having him travel the world every year on the night before Christmas, to deliver a gift of love to every girl and boy. This would not only make all the children happy, but it would also remind them of the true meaning of Christmas. He had also been given the *Gift of Time* to make this task possible.

Kristina knew that *her* wish had been granted. Nicholas and Goe took Kristina to the lodge. She was only the second person to ever visit The Land Beyond Yon. The Elves were all very happy to see her.

Nicholas gave Kristina a grand tour of the lodge. She was very happy to be there, and when they arrived at the Wishroom, where Luigi was working, she was surprised to see all the letters from children around the world. She offered to help sort them out. Nicholas accepted her offer, and each day they would work together.

In the evenings she would read stories to the Elves after dinner.

Nicholas and Kristina became very fond of each other and, as things happen, they fell in love. One day, Nicholas asked her to marry him. Kristina hugged him as she exclaimed, "YES!" They decided to marry on the day before Christmas and they began to make plans for the wedding.

The doll-maker made a beautiful white wedding outfit for her. She also made a new outfit for Nicholas. There was a giant cake, roast beast, cookies, pies, and all sorts of treats. The Elves decorated the walls and tables. Everyone helped to make this a most special event.

Finally, it was December 24th. Goe escorted Kristina down the isle.
Nicholas took her hand and the service began.

42

A few minutes later, the words were spoken, "I now pronounce you husband and wife." They kissed each other and the Elves cheered loudly.

When people married, it was common practice to go on a wedding trip, or honeymoon, as it was commonly called. Nicholas made an announcement: Kristina would be going with him to make the Christmas Eve deliveries. Kristina was delighted! After all, he had told her that he had a wonderful surprise for her.

Later that day, the Elves loaded the sleigh. The newly married couple climbed aboard and Nicholas surprised Kristina by handing her the reins. They both shouted "Up, up and away!" and away they flew. The Elves all cheered and waved as Kristina and Nicholas waved back.

At their first stop, Nicholas climbed down off the sleigh. Kristina handed the gifts to Nicholas and he placed them at the front door, as he had always done. "Are you just going to leave them there?" she asked. "Why not?" he said. Kristina reminded him that they could be damaged by snow or rain or wind, or by any number of things.

Nicholas decided to put the gifts *inside* the home. 47

Kristina loved to fly the sleigh and deliver presents. They visited home after home, and they were enjoying every minute of their trip. After all, both their wishes had come true. But then, *it happened*!

As they visited one of the very last homes, a young child woke up and stepped into the room. The only light came from the glow of the fireplace. Kris was holding the door for Nicholas, as he carried his sack outside. The child wiped his sleepy eyes and asked, "Who are you?"

Kristina looked back at the child and said, "My name is Kris Kringle!
I wish you a *Very* Merry Christmas!"

As the years passed, the child told his story over and over. Some people believed him, and some did not. The fact is, however, that to this very day, every one who *believes*, is filled with the *Spirit of Christmas* and *God's Light* shines upon them. Some people say it's a miracle, some say it's Saint Nicholas, and some say it's Kris Kringle. Some people even think that Kris Kringle and Saint Nicholas are the same person.

But, you know the *real* story, and *I* know it's all true, because *I* was there, the whole time.

53

Acknowledgements

With special thanks to the many special friends and artists who have contributed to the publication of this Limited First Edition of "The Nicholas Stories: The Maiden Voyage of Kris Kringle ".

A special thanks to Harry Knights for the labor of his love, and to Christine Knights, an excellent Elf and special friend, to Betty and Harry Knights Jr. for their loyal and enthusiastic support. To Charlie Flood for staying the course; to Doris Hefler, Phil Testa, Steve Gonzalez, Vincent and Mahrub Neville, Henry Scheuring, Jim and Doris Courchaine and Andrew C. Rigrod, all who in their special way, saw the vision as it turned into reality.

To Tom and Claudia Burton, Joel Fainor, Chavdar Chushev, and, all the Calico Creations' crew, whose beautiful paintings tell a story within our story.

To Hans Kaczmarek, Master German Photographer and Son, whose knowledge of film, the love of art and the persistence to capture the color palette and illumination of our paintings.

To the entire staff of Blackhawk Color Corporation, whose trained eyes and technical expertise brought to life the brilliance of our paintings.

To Lou and JoAnn Rotunno, Patrick and Nancy Keenan, George and Edwina Worsley, Yoshiro and Sueko Oishi, Alison and Beth Donovan, Norman Godheim, Randy DeFazio, Thomas Rotunno, Alan and Jacklyn Schmetzer, Stephanie and Richard Gehring, Rebecca Womble, Elizabeth Rotunno, Mark Mazzone, Linda Hyer, Jill Ressler, Mark Kasrel, Kevin and Karen Hand, Robert and Josephine Tomasulo, Sheila Wessner, Amy McCallum, Rene Gandelman, Michael Long, Brad McKinney, Ralph and Patricia Rotunno, Harriet Segal, Thomas Steele, Mike Brown, Jan Kenny and family, Kathy Gomberg, Al Golden, James Petroff, James Edmonson, Warren Schmidt, Richard and Ellen Stupak, David West, James and Bonnie Parsons, Ross Hagstoc, Henry and Christine Coleman, James McDade, Anthony Latona, Edna Shields, Harold Markle, Steven Passion, Brad Yoder, Leonard Platnick, Marcus Barth, Vito and Jean Magarelli, Robert and Jennifer Carmignani, Dante S. Alberi, Darlene Calzon-Barror, Christopher Ferguson, James Rowe, Lawrence Kirsch, Gerald Weinberg, Alex Fradkoff, Hope Victor, Christopher Carpino, Bruce Moneta, Denise Conti, Arnold Weiss, Craig Martin, Naomi Marcus Zebrick, Tim and Lisa Zuffi, B.J. Fitzgerald, Loretta Conti, Melissa Kopolow, Thomas O'Brien, Vito and Jean Magarelli, Wendy and Andy Johanson, Alena Whitt, Ed Beckett, Michelle Rotunno, Virginia Hobkirk, Linda Kay Hobkirk, Charlotte Morello, Cynthia Patterson, Shirley Fargas, Raymond Smith, Karen Friedman Kravitt, Gregory Zambrycki, George Cantor, Daniel Bowerman, Elaine Axlerod, Peter Moneta, Leonard Danzig, Irvin Smiler, Joan Frey-Boytim, Phyllis Poe Kenny, Suzana & Kendal Schmidt, Margaret and Robert Schmidt, Larry, Laura and Susan Green, Peter Moneta, Robert Bell, Michael Quinlan, Leroy Moyer, Scott Borden, Dolly Friedman, Paul and Lorraine Langenbuch, Mary Ann Horst, Steven Hobkirk, Toby Schmidt, Susan Borden, Edward A. Rosboschil, Anne Oleynick David Kravit, Renate Rotunno, Frank Leto, James O'Brien, Diana Raph, Judith Kuhns, Harry Kaplan, Louis Kopolow, George Graham, Philip Litwak, Stanley Schneider, Audrey Meredith, Steve Napiecek, James O'Brien, James A. Farmer, Harry Quinlan, Michael Tyson, Robert Smith, Wilba Gae and Tom Smith, Brian McGuire, Kenneth C. Welsh, Jr., Pamela Rosenberg, Harvey Spector, Beth Schlein, Donna Moyer, Michael Friedman, Audrey Drenios, David Rotunno, John Churchill, and, David J. Levenson.

In Loving Memory of Roger H. Hefler, co-founder of Studio City Holding, partner and special friend, Henry G. Scheuring, an international gentleman, a loyal friend and multitalented multi-national professional, and, Arthur G. Drenios, a glowing inspiration and innovative financier.

To my guardian angels, Martha, Gurnie and Ona, whose presence lights the path.

And with more thanks than I can express, to Audrey and Lauren, whose love and smiles inspired this publication, and, to Ginny for her relentless love and guiding force.

Larry D. Faw

The Nicholas Stories:

"The Boy With A Wish"

"The First Flight of Saint Nicholas"

"The Maiden Voyage of Kris Kringle"

the end..